Rumblewick's ~~My~~ Diary

My Unwilling Witch
Starts a Girl Band

Hiawyn Oram • Sarah Warburton

LITTLE, BROWN AND COMPANY
New York   Boston

To Lara and "Ribbit Ribbit" Gabe,
with love
H. O.

For Jenny
S. W.

Little, Brown and Company

Hachette Book Group
237 Park Avenue, New York, NY 10017
Visit our website at www.lb-kids.com

Little, Brown and Company is a division of Hachette Book Group,
Inc. The Little, Brown name and logo are trademarks of Hachette Book Group, Inc.

First U.S. Edition: November 2009
First published in Great Britain in 2007 by Orchard Books

ISBN: 978-0-316-03471-5

10 9 8 7 6 5 4 3 2 1

RRD-C

Printed in the United States of America

Contract of Service

between
WITCH HAGATHA AGATHA, Haggy Aggy for short, HA for shortest
of Thirteen Chimneys, Wizton-under-Wold

&

the Witch's Familiar,
RUMBLEWICK SPELLWACKER MORTIMER B, RB for short

It is hereby agreed that, come
FIRE, Brimstone, CAULDRONS overflowing,
or ALIEN WIZARDS invading,
for the NEXT SEVEN YEARS
RB will serve HA,
obey her EVERY WHIM AND WORD and at all times assist her
in the ways of being a true and proper WITCH.

PAYMENT for services will be:
* a log basket to sleep in * unlimited slime buns for breakfast
* free use of HA's broomsticks (outside of peak brooming hours)
* and a cracked mirror for luck.

PENALTY for failing in his duties will be decided on the whim of
THE HAGS on HIGH.

SIGNED AND SEALED
this New Moon Day, 22nd of Remember

Haggy Aggy
....
Witch Hagatha Agatha

Rumblewick
....
Rumblewick Spellwacker Mortimer B

Trixie Fiddlestick
....
And witnessed by the High Hag Trixie Fiddlestick

A SHORT HISTORY
OF HOW YOU COME TO BE READING MY
VERY PRIVATE DIARIES

In a snail shell, they were STOLEN. Oh yes, no less. My witch, Haggy Aggy (HA for short), sneaked into my log basket and helped herself.

According to her, this is what happened:

On one of her many shopping trips to Your Side she met a Book Wiz. (I am told you call them publishers, though Wiz seems more fitting as they make books appear, as if by magic, _every day_ of the _week._)

Anyway, this Book Wiz/publisher wanted HA to write an account of HER life as a witch here on Our Side. Of course, HA wasn't willing to do _that._ Being the most unwilling witch in witchdom, she is far too busy shopping, watching TV, not cackling, being anything BUT a witch, and getting me into trouble with the High Hags* as a result.

The Book Wiz begged on her knees (apparently) and offered HA a life's supply of shoes if she came up with something. So HA did. She came up with THIS — MY DIARIES. ALL OF THEM!!!!

Of course, when I wrote the diaries, I was _not_ expecting anyone to read them. Let alone Othersiders like you. But as you are, here is a word to the wise about how things work between us:

---

* The High Hags run everything around here. They RULE.

1. We are here on THIS SIDE and you are there on the OTHER SIDE.

2. Between us is the HORIZON LINE.

3. You don't see we're here, on This Side, living our lives, because for you the Horizon Line is always a day away. You can walk for a thousand moons (or more for all I know), but you'll never reach it.

4. On the other paw, we know you're there because we visit you all the time. This is partly because of broomsticks. A broomstick has no trouble with any Horizon Line anywhere. A broomstick (with one or more of us upon it) just flies straight through.

And it has to be like that because scaring Otherside children into their wits is part of witches' work. In fact it is Number One on the Witches' Charter of Good Practice (see copy glued at the back).

On the other paw, it is NOWHERE in the Charter for a witch to go over to Your Side to make friends and try to be and do everything you are and do — as my witch, Haggy Aggy, does.

But then, that's my giant problem: being cat to a witch who doesn't want to be one. And as you will see from these diaries, it makes my life a right BAG OF HEDGEHOGS. So all I can say is, if HA tries to make friends with YOU, send her straight back to This Side with a spider in her ear.

Thank you,
Rumblewick Spellwacker Mortimer B. xxx

This Diary Belongs to:

Rumblewick Spellwacker Mortimer B.

RUMBLEWICK for short, RB for shortest

Address:
Thirteen Chimneys,
Wizton-under-Wold, This Side
Bird's Eye View: 331 N by WW

Telephone:
77+3-5+1-7

Nearest Otherside Telephone:
Ditch and Candleberry Bush Street,
N by SE Over the Horizon

Birthday:
Windy Day 23rd Magogary

EDUCATION:
The Awethunder School for Familiars
12-Moon Apprenticeship to the
High Hag Witch Trixie Fiddlestick

QUALIFICATIONS:
Certified Witch's Familiar

CURRENT EMPLOYMENT:
Seven-year contract with Witch Hagatha Agatha,
Haggy Aggy for short, HA for shortest

HOBBIES:
Catnastics, Point-to-Point Shrewing, Languages

NEXT OF KIN:
Uncle Sherbet (retired Witch's Familiar)
Moldy Old Cottage,
Flying Teapot Street,
Prancetown

Dear Diary,

In a zillion moons you will never guess where I am writing this, so I'll tell you — on the Other Side in an enormous bed in the Righton Luxury Beach Hotel!!!

We are here because Haggy Aggy saw it on TV.

"Everyone deserves a lot of luxury once in their lives, RB," she said. "And witches and their Familiars are no exception. Now let's get packing and go."

We did not go at once. In fact, we did not leave for

TWO DAYS
because she couldn't decide what to pack.

Her biggest problem was what to wear on the luxury beach and beside the "dazzling ultramarine" pool.

I mean,
I ask you.

A witch on a beach or beside a pool — luxurious and dazzling or just plain wet and bedraggling? Not in the Witches' Charter of Good Practice, that is for sure.

<u>And</u> if the High Hags see HA in swimwear AT ALL, I know what they will certainly do. They will certainly send me back to First Grade in Witch's Cat School to relearn how to keep my witch from showing her knees and getting herself deep in cold water.

Meanwhile, as I write, HA is downstairs — in her words — enjoying a drink in the Pink Fizz Lounge.

"I shall also be socializing," she said, "which for your edification means making friends with Othersiders. You see, this is what one does when one comes to a luxury beach hotel like the Righton.

It is expected."

She wanted me to socialize with her but I wriggled out of it because of

the stares.

I just had to have a break from the stares.

Everywhere we go in this place, the other Luxury Breakers look at us as if we had three heads. SOCKS! I'll have to hide you. She's at our door, rattling the key card in the key card slot and singing "FLY ME TO THE TOP OF THE HIGHEST TOWER" at the

top of her voice!

Dear Diary,

What a day it has been at the Righton.

After a stare-filled lunch (well, HA's hat WAS bigger than an alien wizard's flying saucer), she was attracted by a sign near the hotel entrance. "Oh, RB!" she cried. "Do look! It's covered in glitzy stars so it must have something **very** important to communicate. Now you read Otherside better than I do, so read it to me, <u>please</u>, <u>at the</u> triple pre<u>sto</u>!"

So I did, and in between the STARS it said:

GIRL BANDS ARE US

WE MAKE THEM **BIG.**
COULD YOU BE OUR NEXT
BIG ONE?
AUDITIONS START AT 3:00 P.M.
IN THE STARSTRUCK ROOM
ON THE FIRST FLOOR.
BE THERE AND BE BIGGER THAN
YOU **EVER DREAMED**
YOU COULD BE.

At that point we did not know what a Girl Band or a Girl Band audition was but HA insisted we go up to the Starstruck Room to find out.

And find out we did: a Girl Band is Otherside girls dressing up (or wearing clothes that nearly fall off), dancing on a shiny platform and singing like their voices just jumped out of their bodies and started dancing too.

An audition is when a Girl Band does all of the above in front of three Othersiders who are called the Producers and Promoters.

When the PPs have watched many Girl Band auditions over many moons, they will choose the band they like best and make it "bigger" than it ever dreamed it could be.

And being **bigger** than you ever

dreamed

you could be means

1 Dancing and singing on TV and shiny platforms all over the universe,

2 Having zillions of your songs heard by Othersiders in what they call ALBUMS,

★ 20 Zillion Album Sales

3 Appearing on pocket-sized TVs that Othersiders keep close at all times (and also use for nonstop talking to OTHER Othersiders probably because they don't have broomsticks to get there and talk for real).

Well, no prizes for guessing what HA is going to do now.

Oh, YES!

The moment we left the Starstruck Room, she announced it.

She is going to start her own Girl Band. And enter it in the next

GIRL BANDS
ARE US

audition in seven days' time!!

WARNING
TOP
SECRET

And here, dear Diary, is where I am going to make a CONFESSION, because that's what diaries are for — admitting the secret thoughts you can't actually admit to anyone else.

So this is it.
My secret confession:

I <u>LIKE</u> GIRL BAND MUSIC.

Up there in the
Starstruck Room it
got me going — my
head ting-zinging and
my paws tap-rapping.

And when my witch announced she was
going to start a Girl Band, I did not think
YUKSTRAW and TRIPLE YIKES, which any
proper Witch's Familiar should think.

I thought EXPLODING SUPERNOVAS and OVER THE MOON. THIS COULD BOIL AND BUBBLE!

Naturally, I did not admit any of this to HA. When we got back to our room, I did what I am trained to do when my witch strays from being a proper witch: I tried to talk her out of it.

"<u>But</u>, Haggy Aggy," I said, "you are not a girl; you are a witch. And witches are witches. They have no business in Girl Bands. And anyway, to start a Girl Band you need other girls. And you don't have any other girls. Or perhaps you are thinking of asking Witch Understairs to join? Or maybe the High Hags?"

She did not notice my SARCASTIC tone, she was so carried away.

"A High Hag is <u>not</u> impossible," she said.

"Especially the High Hag Iodine Underwood. I happen to know she has a BEAUTIFUL singing voice.

"And in any case, I do have other girls for my Girl Band. I have Bella and

I have YOU!"

!! Bella and ME???!

Now it _was_

YIKES AND THRICE YIKES. ??

"BUT," I protested, "Bella is a FROG. A croaky green Clinger! And ME?

I'm a highly qualified Familiar from a long line of highly qualified Familiars.

I AM NOT, and NEVER CAN be, a girl in a Girl Band!"

"Rubbish," said HA. "If there isn't already a spell to turn you into a gorgeous lookalike girl, you will invent one as soon as we get home."

And with that she went to look for more socialization opportunities in the Pink Fizz Lounge, and this time she didn't even ask me to go with her.

00014987

"BORN WITH CLOTHES ON"
LIVE IN CONCERT
At
OLYMPUS STADIUM
Gates Open 5pm - Concert 7.45pm
Dolmat Stand - Upper
BLOCK   ROW   SEAT
   C   O   23
Enter Via Turnstiles 45 to 50

Back Home at Thirteen Chimneys

Dear Diary,

We are back home from the Righton
and the situation has not improved
a tiddly tadpole.

HA is out right now at a concert by
a Girl Band called BORN WITH
CLOTHES ON. A Girl Band that is
apparently already "big."

And guess what? She's only taken — not
me but — Bella!

"I need to see what 'big' is," she said.
"And what 'big' wears. And I'm taking
Bella because SHE has such a
good eye for style."

(A good eye for a
bubbling, boiling cauldron
if you ask me. I mean,
you should SEE how that
frog slimes up to HA.)

"But don't worry, RB," she went on, "while we are gone there is SO MUCH for you to do. First you are to come up with a spell to turn yourself into a Girl Band Girl Lookalike. And when you've done that I want you to come up with a dazzling NAME for our band and write us

a WINNING SONG

for our audition. And I know you will because that's what you do — whatever I ask of you."

Well, what a nest of
nettles! It IS in my Contract
of Service to obey my
witch's every whim
and word, come fire,
brimstone, or alien
wizards invading.

But there is just <u>NO</u> <u>WAY</u> I am <u>EVER</u>
going to be a GIRL in a GIRL BAND.

I mean, I ask you. Leaving out
what the High Hags would do
if they caught me,

I HAVE

<u>MY</u>

<u>PRIDE</u>.

But don't worry, Diary, an idea is coming to me. Yes, here it comes winging its way like a screech owl:

I'll invent a
Girl Lookalike spell
in TWO LAYERS.

One layer for HA's eyes with a second layer that is the REAL SPELL — INVISIBLE unless you know it's there.

And the under layer — where the ACTUAL SPELL lies — will do the following: it will turn the One To Be Spelled (in this case me, worst luck) into a Girl Lookalike all right — a Girl Lookalike whom HA wouldn't want in her Girl Band if she was the last girl in the world!!!

BRILLIANT —

if I do say so myself.

Dear Diary,

I've done it — though it hasn't

yet been tested because someone else has
to perform it on me. (Invented like
that so HA can never accuse me
of not performing it
properly on myself,
on purpose.)

Here is the top layer that covers the real spell:

THE LOOK-LIKE-A-GIRL-BAND-GIRL SPELL

Drape the shoulders of the OTBS (One To Be Spelled) with a pink feather thing. Stand in your hat wearing a pair of high teeterers and holding a cracked mirror. Turn a full circle three times without falling over while turning the cracked mirror to face the OTBS and chanting:

Who looks on you will look and see
A girl in leggings tight
Whose face and legs and arms and all
Are such a pretty sight
For when I step out from this hat
You'll give a girlish twirl
And those who look will look and see
A GORGEOUS GIRL BAND GIRL!

SMALL PRINT: This is a First-Chance-Last-Chance spell.
If it doesn't work the first time, it never will and no other
Look-Like-a-Girl-Band-Girl spell will either.
Bad luck, but that's magic for you.

REVERSAL NOTE: Easy reversal is built into this spell.
To reverse at any time, the One Who Has Been Spelled should sneeze
three times at the moon and shout his/her full name followed by THAT TIS I.

And here is the secret "under layer" — where the <u>REAL</u> spell and its workings lie!

THE LOOK-LIKE-A-GIRL-BAND-GIRL SPELL

WHO LOOKS LIKE A TOAD IN TIGHT LEGGINGS

Drape the shoulders of the OTBS (One To Be Spelled) with a pink feather thing. Stand in your hat wearing a pair of high teeterers and holding a cracked mirror. Turn a full circle three times without falling over while turning the cracked mirror to face the OTBS and chanting:

Who looks on you will look and see
A girl in leggings tight
Whose face and legs and arms and all
Are not a pretty sight
For when I step out from this hat
Though in a girl-like mode
Who looks on you will more likely see
A TIGHTLY TROUSERED TOAD!

SMALL PRINT: This is a First-Chance-Last-Chance spell.
If it doesn't work the first time, it never will and no other
Look-Like-a-Girl-Band-Girl spell will either. Bad luck, but that's magic for you.

Did I hear you say, "Good work, RB," Diary? I think I did.

And that done, I can get on with the thrills and spills part — coming up with a supernova name and writing a winning song for a Girl Band that, thankfully, I'll never be in!!

So, the name?

The name,

the name,

the name???

I heard the GIRL BANDS ARE US Producers and Promoters say they are looking for something different. Well, nothing could be more different than HA's Girl Band as it's not a GIRL Band.

It's a Witch and Frog Band with maybe a High Hag or two in it. So why not hit them with the truth, which is always bigger than anything else.

SO, POSSIBLE NAMES FOR
HA'S GIRL BAND:

The Witch, the Frog and the High Hag(s)

The Toadstools

The Potions

The Spell Sisters

The Fireflies

Boil and Bubble

the Spell Sisters

Boiling It Big

Cold Comfrey

The Witch Watch

The Hey Prestos

SPELLSISTERS

The Wizton Wonders

the Potions

The Wizton Wailers

The Crooning Coven

Bubbling Over

THE FIREFLIES

All in Black

The Blue Moons

Once in a Blue Moon*

Witch's whiskers! Now that would work getting her back into black...

No Ordinary Girls

The Never Ever Girls

Forever Witches

The Cauldron Stirrers

~~No Ordinary Girls~~ (got that already)

Bewitching Sisters

The Fire and Brimstones

Oh, SOCKS.

This is fun and there's the doorbell!

Continue soon.

*I like this

me and GRIMEY!

Dear Diary,

My best friend, Grimey — that's who
it was.

Total moon that he is, when I'd told him
the whole Girl Band saga, he offered to
help me invent a winning song.

Of course neither of us had invented
a song before, but we decided it couldn't be
that different from inventing a spell.
And as it turned out,
                    it wasn't.

First we decided we had to sing about something that mattered to us. And, as he is my greatest friend in the universe and I am his, what better than <u>that</u> for a song subject — friendship???

So we dusted down a witch's horn and a gawbox that have been under the sofa for moons.

I dug out my school washboard. We turned over a few cauldrons to drum on with stirring sticks and LET IT HAPPEN.
And I have to admit,
I can't remember when I've enjoyed myself MORE!!

This is what we came up with.
It's called BE RIGHT THERE:

A friend's a friend you have to win
Now I have through thick and thin
You'll be my friend, my total moon,
    I'll be right there
        whatever —

If you feel blue I won't be too
I'll dig right in and root for you
If you need time to be alone
I'll keep away and stay at home

If you are riding far too high
And lose your way, I'll come, I'll fly
    And be right there
        be right there, be right there
            whatever —

A friend's a friend you have to win
Now I have, through thick and thin
You'll be my friend, my total moon,
    I'll be right there
        whatever —

If you have crossed a line too far
And can't remember what you are
If you have fallen in a hole
To get you out will be my role

If every spell you do goes wrong
And you can't see where you belong
I'll be right there
        be right there, be right there
                whatever —

A friend's a friend you have to win
Now I have, through thick and thin
You'll be my friend
I'll be right there
        be right there, be right there
                forever!

WHAT DO YOU THINK??

Anyway, got to go — by the sound of it,
HA and the Clinger are home!

Much Later, in My Log Basket

Dear Diary,

Well, this is what happens when a Familiar and his witch get carried away with business that is not their business, like songwriting and Girl Bands: Trouble comes knocking.

In this case Trouble in the form of the High Hag Iodine Underwood — the one with the beautiful singing voice.

First, though, before she arrived, HA and the Clinger came dancing in through the door full of the songs they'd heard at the concert and what HA is going to wear as the No. 1 singer in her own Girl Band!

And wait for it, Diary. Wait for it.

BLACK.

Oh yes, no less. HA has discovered that black is big in Girl Bands — and now she's talking as if she never said, "Black is yesterday, pink is the new black." Now she has packed all her pink in her flying trunk and sent it to the broomstick shed!!!

She told me to go get some black, which she quickly cut about with the kitchen scissors, pulled on some cliff-high white boots, and there she was looking all

Girl Bandish
back in
black!!!

I couldn't believe it. <u>THEN</u>, when I got out my list of possible names for her band, she didn't even LOOK at it.

"Don't worry, RB," she said. "Flying home from the concert, Bella and I came up with the dazzling band name we need. It's <u>obvious</u>, isn't it:

'BACK IN BLACK'!!"

They were so excited they did not
see my disappointment that my list of names
was not needed or listen when
I said, "That's almost the name I was going
to suggest."

HA did not ask if I'd invented a Look-
Like-a-Girl-Band-Girl spell. NOR
did she ask if I'd written
a winning song. Why? Because she
and Bella had not only come up
with the name for the band
on their way back from
the concert — but
they had a song
too.

"And it's so HOT it's MAGMA!"
cried HA. "LISTEN!"

Well, you could have knocked me over with a pink feather thing. HA was right. Their song boiled and bubbled. It steamed. It WAS magma — straight from the volcano's mouth! I could just hear it winning any audition and making HA bigger than she'd ever DREAMED she could be.

It goes like this:

BELLA: RIBBIT, RIBBIT

HA: YOU CAN'T INHIBIT..................ME

BELLA: RIBBIT, RIBBIT...

HA: STAR EXHIBIT..................ME
         Like a star in the heavens
         I'm a light on the ground
         My time's been a-coming
         Now my time's come around

BELLA: RIBBIT, RIBBIT, RIBBIT, RIBBIT

HA: Yeah, I'm hot, hot rocking
         In my little black dress
         If the world is watching
         I can only confess ...

BELLA: RIBBIT, RIBBIT — CAN'T INHIBIT ...
         HER RIBBIT, RIBBIT ...

```
BOTH:     STAR EXHIBIT.....................ME/HER
          Yeah . . . we're hot, hip-hopping
          In our high, high heels
          Let the world get watching
          And know how it feels . . .
          RIBBIT, RIBBIT
          RIBBIT, RIBBIT — STAR EXHIBIT . . .

HA:       ME!
```

When they'd finished I was so amazed,
I didn't know what to say. And it didn't
matter because this was the moment when
Trouble/the High Hag Iodine Underwood
rapped on the window and demanded to
be let in!

Oh! What's this? It's Bella the Clinger
hopping toward my basket, sobbing
a pond. I'll go on later —

if I don't <u>drown</u> in her <u>tears.</u>

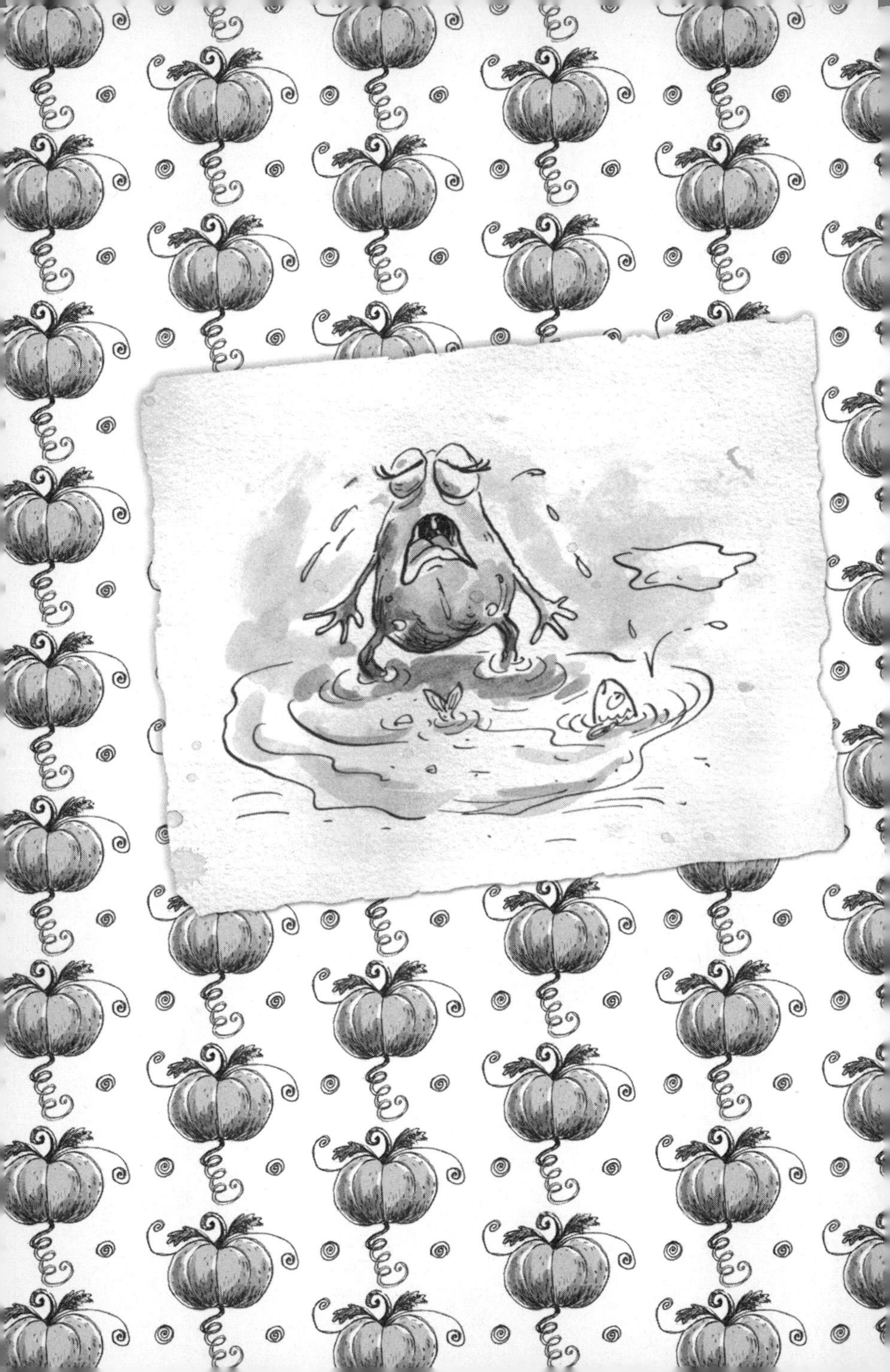

Nearly Dawning Time and Sorry If You're Soaked

Dear Diary,

Bella was sobbing a pond because she isn't going to be in HA's Girl Band after all — but I'll come to that in a moment.

Meanwhile, back to the entrance of the High Hag Iodine Underwood.

I smelled wet rot immediately — because it turned out she hadn't come to roast HA for hot, hot rocking in a little black dress — or me for letting her.

She'd heard the singing on her way to take comfrey tea with Witch Understairs next door. Said she hadn't let her voice out for moons and could she JOIN IN?????

So join in she did. And blow me down
with a feather thing again, can she sing?!
She can belt it out and rock with the best.
She can also play the horn and the gawbox!
    And with me on the cauldron drums,
Thirteen Chimneys was soon jumping so
hard its Thirteen Chimneys

were rocking too.

When we'd done $\boxed{\text{STAR}}$ $\boxed{\text{EXHIBIT}}$ a few times, Underwood announced, "One song doesn't make a band, Hagatha dear. So do you have anything else original we can sing?"

HA pointed at me and said, "RB has invented a winning song,

HAVE YOU NOT,

BECAUSE I <u>TOLD YOU TO</u>."

So I sang through BE RIGHT
THERE and even HA thought it was
pretty hot. By the time we'd sung it
together a few times, Witch Understairs
and Grimey arrived to find out what was
going on. So did all the frogs from the
frog pen, all the eavesdroppers AND Witch
Rattle and her friend Witch Sideways PLUS
their Familiars, Arbuthnot Butnot and Magic
Galore — on their way home from the Blue
Moon Comfrey Rooms.

And everyone agreed on this: we were
too good
to waste.

Too good not to be heard by a wider audience. And would we PLEASE perform at the next Witches' Conference and every Witches' Jamboree forever???

At this point I saw the Trouble we were in showing itself like the mouth of a deep abyss.

HA started to sheer.

Sheer at the very idea that her Girl Band was meant for witches' conferences and jamborees — and not for much bigger things like winning the Girl Bands Are Us competition and disappearing from witchdom forever because she'd become an Otherside Girl Band so big it was galaxy-sized!

Luckily, Underwood stopped her before she really got started. "Oh, thank you everyone for your high praise indeed. But, as a High Hag, I can NEVER be seen performing in a Girl Band. The other High Hags would consider it silly and therefore

x

undermining High Hag authority and for SILLY and UNDERMINING HIGH HAG AUTHORITY, a High Hag is sent spinning into The Blue That Lies Beyond All. So now I'll put my voice back in its box and we'll forget this evening ever happened!"

With that she cast
a cloud of Polished Talon
Dust about the room to make
us forget what we'd seen.

HA and I were quick
enough to avoid any of it
falling on us. But the dust
showered down on the others,
and as soon as Underwood had left, they
started wondering what they
were doing in our house.

HA sent them home with no
explanation other than "witnessing
the birth of BACK IN BLACK," which made
as much sense to them as if she'd said

JIBBLES and JIRASOLES.

And as soon as we were on our own,

HA exploded

with excitement — and I saw

just how deep the Abyss of Trouble

was that we were

about to fall into.

"Oh, RB, Bella . . .
        don't you see . . ."
            she cried.

"I've found the other girl for my Girl
Band. It's HER. Iodine Underwood!
She sings like a skylark. And she
hot-rocks too. With that voice and my
voice, BACK IN BLACK can't fail
to become galaxy-sized. Now, here's the
challenge. How are we going to make her
look NOT like the horrendous old Hag she is
but a gorgeous Girl Band Girl?"

She paced about in her cliff-high
boots and then spun around and
pointed at me.

"Easy. Of course.
While we were at the
concert, you came up
with a LOOK-LIKE-A-
GIRL-BAND-GIRL SPELL.

Didn't you?

Because if not,

why <u>not</u>?"

The spell — with its double
layers — was lying on the kitchen table.
I tried to get to it, thinking . . . turning a
High Hag into a girl that looks like a toad
in tight leggings WOULD NOT BE A GOOD
MOVE for a witch and her Familiar.
But HA's beady eyes went ahead of me.
   "Of course, you did. Because you are the
                 most faithful Familiar
                     ever to come out
                        of Familiar
                        School."
                        And she
                        pounced
                       on it. And
                    flicked through
                it — naturally seeing
            only its
            surface layer.

"Tempests and treacle, this will do the trick perfectly!"

she declared. "Now all I have to do is visit High Hags' Headquarters and perform it on Iodine. Thank you, RB."

"But-but-but," I stammered.

"You mustn't.

You can't.

That spell has . . . I don't think it's . . . it hasn't been tested."

"So now we'll test it," said HA. "Bring me a super-speedy broomstick that I won't feel sick on, RB. I must do this alone."

"No, no, HA," I argued. "It's too dangerous. If the other High Hags find a Girl Band Girl Lookalike in their Headquarters, what'll they do? Find out who put her there — YOU — and chase you into the byways and back alleys of witchdom, or worse: turn me into a cauldron <u>toad</u> for <u>letting</u> you!"

"And, and," added Bella, coming to my aid without knowing it, "if Iodine Underwood finds herself looking like a Girl Band girl lookalike, she'll know exactly who did it to her because of tonight."

"Right," I said. "Bella is right and so am I. Forget about the High Hag Iodine Underwood in your Girl Band."

"Besides," said Bella, "you don't need her. You have ME. And if you perform that spell on RB, you have him."

But HA was so carried away with herself as a galaxy-sized Girl Band, she forgot not to be cruel.

"YOU?" she almost cackled at Bella. "YOU? Compared to Iodine Underwood you don't sing. You <u>croak</u>. And as for you, RB, I've had second thoughts about you being in my band. You'll be far more useful taking care of us. Making sure we're produced and promoted right. Maybe inventing some more songs.

And becoming — how shall I put it — Back In Black's Manager Cat."

And here she presented me with a pair of eye shades, which she must have purchased at the Righton Beach Shop.

I put them on and have to confess again: a <u>thrill</u> went through me.

My head spun.

Back in Black's manager???

In eye shades. Strolling about in the Starstruck Room, negotiating my Girl Band's future with PPs?

Was this my <u>destiny</u> after all?

If it was, it wasn't crusty old vinegar.

Not crusty old vinegar at <u>all</u>!

GALAXY-SIZED
GIRL BAND
MANAGER
OF THE YEAR

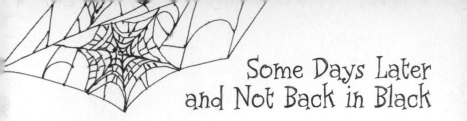

Dear Diary,

What webs we tangle ourselves in as soon as
we try to be what we aren't. All I can say
is I hope what has happened will be
a lesson to me.

As soon as I put on those Righton Shop
eye shades and thrilled at the thought of
being Back in Black's manager, I was sliding
well into the

Abyss of Trouble.

And sliding fast.

First, it came over me that HA was right.
Iodine Underwood DID sing like
a skylark who also rocks. HA is good
and could pass for a gorgeous Girl
Band girl any day. But to win the
GIRL BANDS ARE US competition
we HAD to have Iodine in our
band. (OUR band — note the
slippery slide.) And as its new
manager (in eye shades), I'd do
anything to get her.

So, cool as a cauldron of
hailstones, I told HA the truth about
that Girl Lookalike spell. And then
reconfigured the spell —

at the presto —

to take out its <u>second</u> layer
and make it work on its <u>surface</u> layer!!

By the time I'd done that I'd thought of a way for HA to convince Iodine to join BACK IN BLACK (once she was looking like a gorgeous Girl Band girl).

"Just warn her,"

I said, "that if she refuses, you'll tell the other High Hags she

rocked

the night away at Thirteen Chimneys and she'll soon be sent SPINNING INTO THE BLUE THAT LIES BEYOND ALL."

Then I gave HA our speediest broomstick and wished her well on her mission.

What was I thinking,
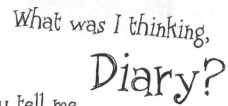

Diary?

You tell me.

Because HA did just that. And soon returned with Iodine on the back of her broomstick looking GORGEOUS in her own little black dress.

We kept her rehearsing here at Thirteen Chimneys (with plenty of reminders of The Blue That Lies Beyond All) until the day arrived for the auditions at the Starstruck Room.

Bella and I hung around at the back (I'd made her my assistant to help with her disappointment at not being in the band).

She tried not to hop with impatience and I tried not to twirl OFF my Lucky Whisker with excitement while we waited.

Finally, our wait was over. Last but not least, HA and Iodine took the stage and performed our

two

magma-<u>hot</u>

songs —

BE RIGHT THERE

and

STAR EXHIBIT.

I only wish you could have seen those Producers and Promoters and the rest of the audience when BACK IN BLACK had finished. They leapt to their feet. They wept. They clapped.

One PP cried out:

"IF EVER A GIRL BAND DESERVES TO BE BIGGER THAN THEIR DREAMS IT'S YOU!"

But this is where we hit rock bottom of the Abyss of Trouble.

To fully understand why, go back to the EASY REVERSAL NOTE for that Look-Like-a-Girl-Band-Girl spell I invented — because reversal was

WHAT WAS about to happen!

"Now," said the first
PP, pointing at HA. "You
are Hagatha Agatha." Then
pointing at Iodine, "and you
are..."

At that moment THE MOON
APPEARED AT A WINDOW.

Iodine glanced at it — SNEEZED
THREE TIMES without knowing
what she was doing — and answered
the PP in all innocence:

"IODINE UNDERWOOD. THAT TIS I!"

And it WAS HER!

The Look-Like-a-Girl-Band-Girl spell
reversed in a flash — and there was
Iodine — a full-on High Hag.

At the sight of it, and her Girl Band dreams going up in the smoke of truth,

HA fell down in a swoon.

Panic broke out in the Starstruck Room.

Though not for long: realizing she was revealed to so many for what she is, Iodine went RIGHT OVER THE TOP with the Polished Talon Dust so no one would remember what they'd seen.

This time Bella and I escaped it by hiding under a chair — but a whole cloud fell on the helpless Haggy Aggy, swooning on the floor. So much in fact that for two days she hasn't been able to remember her own name.

Of course, I'm taking great care of her and feeding her Begoneberry Broth to begone the effects of all that

Forgetfulness Dust.

I don't know what she will have to say when she fully recovers. I'm hoping she will remember everything and not give a gawbox that she nearly became a GALAXY-SIZED Girl Band. I'm hoping what happened in the Starstruck Room will teach her a lesson too about staying true to what you are — in her case a witch and a very good one, if only she'd be more willing.

As for me. I mean, I ask you.
A GIRL BAND MANAGER? As I keep
asking of myself in adazement: What
WAS I thinking of? I'm a Highly Qualified
Witch's Familiar from a long line of Witch's
Familiars. That's what
I am and that's what I always will be.

Mind you,
   I don't see
   why I can't be
that which I am —

IN MY SUPERNOVA
      NEW EYE SHADES.
                Can you?

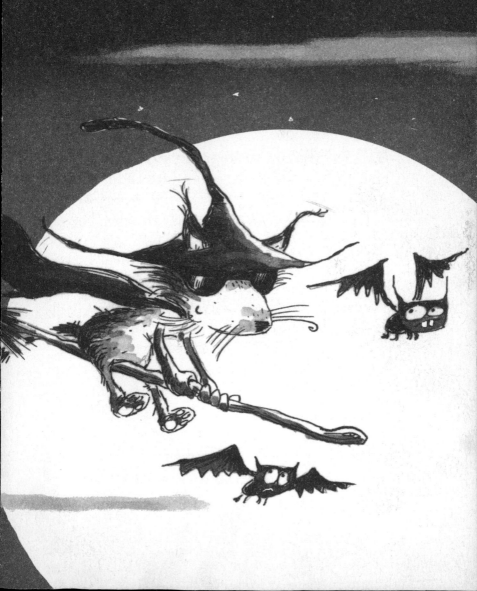

WITCHES' CHARTER
OF GOOD PRACTICE

1. Scare at least one child on the Other Side into his or her wits — every day (excellent), once in seven days (good), once a moon (average), once in two moons (bad), once in a blue moon (failed).

2. Identify any fully grown Othersiders who were not properly scared into their wits as children and DO IT NOW. (It is never too late for a grown Othersider to come to his or her senses.)

3. Invent a new spell useful for every purpose and every occasion in the Witches' Calendar. Ensure that you or your Familiar commits it to a spell book before it is lost to the Realms of Forgetfulness forever.

4. Keep a proper witch's house at all times — filled with dust and spiders' webs, mold, and earwigs' underthings; and ensure that the jars on your kitchen shelves are always alive with good spell ingredients.

5. Cackle a lot. Cackling can be heard far and wide and serves many purposes such as (i) alerting others to your terrifying presence and (ii) sounding hideous and thereby comforting to your fellow witches.

6. Make sure your Familiar keeps your means of proper travel (broomsticks) in good repair and that one, either, or both of you exercise them regularly.

7. Never fail to present yourself anywhere and everywhere in full witch's uniform (i.e., black everything and no ribbons upon your hat ever). Sleeping in uniform is recommended as a means of saving dressing time.

8. Keep your Familiar happy with a good supply of comfrey tea and slime buns. Remember, behind every great witch is a well-fed Familiar.

9. At all times acknowledge the authority of your local High Hags. As their eyes can move 360 degrees and they know everything there is to know, it is always in your interests to make their wishes your commands.

Can't get enough of Rumblewick's diaries?
Check out *My Unwilling Witch Gets a Makeover*

Available
February 2010

Here's a note from
Rumblewick about
Haggy Aggy's
latest antics:

Dear Reader,

I'm going totally bats on a broomstick! I thought Haggy was back in
black for good when she wanted to be a rock star, but now she's in
top-to-toe pink! What sort of witch wears PINK?! As if that weren't
enough, she's gone to the Other Side to get a makeover to help jumpstart
her modeling career—and all on Fright Night, no less!

I'm Haggy Aggy's right-hand cat, contractually bound to shape her into
the best broom-wielding, frightfully awful witch she can be, so why must
Haggy prefer tutus and nail polish to black hats and toad spells?

If the Hags on High hear about her antics, I'm toast! You're all I've got,
dear reader—HELP!

TURN THE PAGE FOR A SNEAK PEEK!

Very sincerely,

Rumblewick Spellwacker Mortimer B.

Dear Diary,

The hurtling cloud was her. As it turns out, she hasn't been near Witch Rattle's Bad Temper Competition. ("Oh, RB," she defended herself, "why should I? I always win. Witch Rattle and her friends wouldn't know a Bad Temper if it knocked them off their broomsticks.")

Instead, she's been shopping on the Other Side. And I'm sorry to say, but this is what she's been shopping for:

ROSE, PEACH, GERANIUM, CARNATION,

PALE, SHOCKING, TOADSTOOL,

PENICILLIN, CAT'S TONGUE,

BAT'S TONGUE — whatever — PINK.

Skirts, tiddly tops, dresses, stockings, petticoats, hats, shoes, buckles, bangles, and neckwear —

ALL IN PINK!

She's already packed all her black into her flying trunk and made me send it to the broomstick shed.

"OUT OF MY SIGHT, RB!"

she said.

"BLACK IS YESTERDAY.

PINK IS THE NEW BLACK!"

I tried to reason with her. "But witches wear black," I said. "It's what they do. It's UNIFORM. There's never been a witch in witchdom in top-to-toe pink."

"Well, why not?" she said. "What's

wrong with a witch in pink?

I adore pink."

With that she opened a box of cocoalots topped with PINK sugar roses she'd bought on her PINK shopping spree, turned on Otherside TV, and flung herself onto the sofa like a giant pink powder puff.

I pushed a cup of comfrey tea and a slime bun in front of her — in the midge-sized hope she'd choose them over Otherside rose-topped cocoalots — and went outside in a snit to feed the frogs.

Of course, unlike every other witch in the universe, <u>SHE</u> does not keep frogs for the cauldron.

Make Me Over

Oh no, not my Haggy Aggy. Since she decided to disallow all living creatures from our potions, she (or rather we, as I do all the work) keep them as PETS! And, as every frog in Wizton knows this, each night more sneak into our frog run trying to look like they've always been there.

I was busy shooing today's sneak-ins
back into the woods when Bella leaped onto
my hat. She started kissing me all over

(YUKKLE!)

and promising to do anything I asked of
her if I'd let her come inside
and watch TV with
Haggy Aggy.

I was just saying,
NO — IF I LET YOU,
THEN ALL THE FROGS WILL WANT
TO COME AND WATCH TV TOO,
when HA started yelling "RB! Come
at once. You just have to see this!"
So, with Bella still clinging like
a frog-shaped leech, I went
back inside.

"This" was an Otherside Beauty Program and HA was bouncing about on the sofa screaming, "LOOK, RB! I can't believe it! It's such a lucky meeting of coincidences! They're giving that Othersider a makeover! AND THAT'S WHAT I NEED, RB — AND THAT'S WHAT I'M GOING TO GET — A TOTAL MAKEOVER. Do you know why? I'll tell you. SO I CAN BECOME AN OTHERSIDE SUPERMODEL AND BE ADMIRED ALL OVER THE UNIVERSE FOR MY BEAUTEOUSNESS!"

YIKES AND TRIPLE YIKES

was all I could think.

A witch — MY witch — wanting to be ADMIRED ALL OVER THE UNIVERSE FOR HER BEAUTY?

I shook my ears for webs and earwig nests. Was I hearing right? I was, because next she opened one of her new pink handbags and handed me a printed card picked up on her shopping spree. Here it is for your EDIFICATION:

TIPS FOR BECOMING A
MAGMA-HOT ROCKER AND QUEEN BEE
OF THE GIRLIEST GIRL BAND:

1. Brainstorm for a DAZZLING NAME.

2. Write a WINNING SONG.

3. DRESS THE PART

4. HIRE A FAMILIAR to do the hard stuff for you.

5. CAST A SPELL on the audience.

6. Get your FRIENDS to join you!

7. Make sure you have some loyal FANFROGS.

8. Learn to PLAY AN INSTRUMENT.

9. Wear SHADES.

10. LET YOUR STAR POWER SHINE!

Are you a Rumble-like, a Hag-a-lot, or truly Otherside?

Take this QUIZ and find out!

My favorite girl band is:

A. one I can dance and sing along to.
B. the one I'm the star of.
C. I prefer boy bands.

If I met a witch, I would:

A. teach her a new spell.
B. Who wants to meet a witch? I'd rather go shopping.
C. make her teach me to fly.

If I had a million dollars, I would spend it:

A. on a lifetime supply of slimebuns.
B. on a lifetime supply of pink shoes.
C. on candy (I don't even want to *know* what's in a slimebun—EW!).

The best sleepover activity is:

A. crashing the party.
B. jumping on the bed in my jimjams.
C. playing Truth or Dare.

Mostly A's:

You're a lot like Rumblewick the cat. You're a star student and like to play by the rules, but you know how to head-bop to the music as well as anyone, and you're always there for your friends.

Mostly B's:

You're more like Haggy Aggy. So what if you don't want to be a witch? It's way more fun to be a regular girl! You may have a bit of a temper, but you've got real star power and charisma.

Mostly C's:

You're perfectly happy being Otherside. You're curious about what's beyond the horizon line and would love to meet a real live witch, but you'd rather cheer for the band than be up on stage, and while you LOVE cats, you'd never want to deal with the High Hags in real life!

D	B	R	O	O	M	S	T	I	C	K	T
O	W	H	I	C	H	O	G	W	C	H	S
G	F	C	I	S	X	T	A	I	Z	U	J
H	A	G	G	Y	P	H	W	I	T	C	H
T	M	S	L	I	M	E	B	U	N	S	Q
A	I	O	O	M	L	R	L	H	A	G	S
D	L	I	H	B	G	S	Y	L	X	G	O
O	I	O	M	A	J	I	M	J	A	M	S
F	A	U	O	W	G	D	P	H	U	I	R
T	R	Z	G	D	E	E	H	T	E	L	L
E	F	K	T	M	M	G	P	T	I	C	K
L	V	A	R	R	I	V	O	O	M	L	W
L	C	J	I	H	H	X	S	W	I	C	K

RUMBLEWICK   HIGH HAGS

SLIMEBUNS   WITCH

JIMJAMS   TAD OF TELL

HAGGY   CAT

SPELL   BROOMSTICK

FAMILIAR   OTHERSIDE

Dear Precious Children,

The Publisher asked me to say something about these Diaries.
(As I do not write Otherside very well, I have dictated it to
the Publisher's Familiar/assistant. If she has not written it
down right, let me know and I'll turn her into a fat pumpkin.)

This is my message: I went to a lot of trouble to steal these
Diaries for you. And the Publisher gave me a lot of shoes
in exchange. If you do not read them the Publisher may
want the shoes back. So please, for my sake — the only
witch in witchdom who isn't willing to scare you for her own
entertainment — ENJOY THEM ALL.
Yours ever,

Haggy Aggy

Your fantabulous shoe-loving friend,
Hagatha Agatha (Haggy Aggy for short, HA for shortest) xx